Daredevil

D1321768

LONDON BOROUGH OF BARNET

NIGEL HINTON

Daredevil

Barrington Stoke

First published in 2015 in Great Britain by
Barrington Stoke Ltd
18 Walker Street, Edinburgh, EH3 7LP

www.barringtonstoke.co.uk

Text © 2015 Nigel Hinton

The moral right of Nigel Hinton to be identified as the author of this work has been asserted in accordance with the Copyright, Designs and Patents Act, 1988

All rights reserved. No part of this publication may be reproduced in whole or in any part in any form without the written permission of the publisher

A CIP catalogue record for this book is available
from the British Library upon request

ISBN: 978-1-78112-436-9

Printed in China by Leo

Contents

Chapter 1
The Break-up

I know Sam never liked me. But that wasn't why he made me do the dares. He was wild and he could be cruel, but I don't think he wanted to hurt me or get me into real trouble. He couldn't have known what was going to happen.

No, I think Sam made me do the dares because he loved me. That sounds weird, but it's true – I think you can love someone even if you don't like them. Brothers love each other, don't they? But they don't have to like each other. Me, I love Sam. Always have done, no matter what he did to me.

My big brother Sam. Three years older than me. I always looked up to him. He was strong and good at sports and I suppose he was my hero.

I wanted to be like him – but I wasn't. He wanted a brother he could play football and rugby and cricket with, and I was no good at those things.

"Come on, Ben – you can do it," he always said when he tried to teach me to play football. And I'd really try, but the ball would just trickle away or fly off the wrong way and Sam would groan.

It was the same with cricket and tennis. I could never hit the ball properly and Sam hated that.

"Why are you so crap at sport?" he said one day when I tried to trap the football and fell over.

"I'm good at swimming," I told him.

"So are fish. Big deal! You're just a wimp," Sam said and went off to wait for Dad to come home.

Dad was good at everything that Sam loved. He played for the local rugby club and Sam did too. In the evenings or at weekends, Dad and Sam were always together – playing sports, going on training runs, working on Sam's bike or Dad's motorbike, mucking about and laughing together.

So when Mum and Dad split up, Sam wanted to live with Dad.

I was nine and I just sat there and cried when Mum and Dad told us they didn't want to be together any more. Sam didn't cry. He got up and went and stood next to Dad. It was like he was picking sides for a game in the playground. It was horrible.

But Sam wasn't allowed to choose to be on Dad's side. Mum told us that we were both going to live with her during the week and stay with Dad at weekends.

Chapter 2
Chicken

Sam looked forward to the weekends with Dad, but I hated them. It was sport, sport, sport from morning to night. Rugby in the winter, cricket in the summer – and I had to watch. I hated watching Dad play. He was good but he always had this fierce look on his face as if sport was some kind of war.

Sam was different. He made everything look easy and fun. He was like a dancer. A little swerve to the left or the right and he would duck away from a tackle in rugby and dive for the line to score a try. And in cricket he always seemed to have so much time, no matter how fast someone bowled at him. A little shuffle, a flick of his wrist, and the ball would fly exactly where he wanted it.

Dad played with a frown on his face. Sam played with a smile on his.

I would have preferred just to watch, but one day Dad decided that he wanted me to play too. He made me join the rugby club and train with them twice a week.

There were two games when the club's junior team was short of players and I got picked. In the first game I didn't get near the ball but, in the second one, someone passed the ball to me and I started to run with it. I could hear Dad and Sam shouting as I ran towards the line. Then a big player from the other team hit me with a hard tackle and knocked me to the ground.

"Don't just lie there, Ben – get on with it!" Dad shouted.

I was winded and my ribs hurt but I got up and the game went on.

Two minutes later I got the ball again. I ran towards the line and saw the same player rush forward to tackle me. I panicked and threw the ball away, hoping it would look like a pass. But it just dropped to the ground and the big player from the other team picked it up, ran down the field and scored a try.

"I know you're small," Dad said after the game, "but that's no excuse to chicken out of a tackle. Have you ever seen me or Sam do that? No. You need to man up, Ben."

On the way home in the car, Sam turned round and said, "Chick Chick Chicken!" Dad laughed and Sam made some clucking noises. From then on, "Chick" was Sam's nickname for me.

I was never picked for the rugby team again. Part of me was pleased, but I was ashamed, too – ashamed that Dad thought I was a coward.

I asked Mum if I could stay with her at weekends, but she said Dad would be upset.

"No, he won't," I said. "He thinks I'm chicken."

"Don't be silly – of course he doesn't," Mum said. "He loves you, Ben. I know he's sports mad and you're not, but just show him all the things you can do. Make him proud of what you *are* good at."

So I started to take my drawing pad along when I went to watch the games. Dad looked at it one day and said he liked one of the sketches

I'd done of a cricket match. I tore it out and gave it to him.

"I'll put that on the fridge door," he promised.

But he never did.

Chapter 3
Out of My Way

The day I started at Sam's school, he pushed me against the wall in the playground. "Stay out of my way, Chick," he said. "Got it? If you embarrass me in front of my mates I'll smash your face in."

I nodded. And I did try to stay out of his way. But if he ever saw me in the corridor he'd always give me a sly punch or try to trip me up.

I hated him when he did that, but then the next day he might do or say something nice and it would make me happy again. If he was in a good mood he could be kind and funny and I would forgive him for all the times he bullied me.

It was the same with Mum. Sam would be rude and bad tempered and push her until she almost lost it. Then he would smile and put his arm round her and you could see her anger melt away.

But he couldn't get round her so easily when he started to get into trouble at school.

Sam had never liked school but there were never any real problems until he fell in with a gang of boys who scared everyone – even some of the teachers. From then on he was always on report and Mum kept being called in to talk about his bad conduct and his poor work.

"What's got into you, Sam?" Mum asked after yet another meeting with the Head Teacher. "You didn't used to be like this. You should be setting a good example to Ben."

Sam glared at me as if it was my fault and I wondered if it was. Was he acting up because I was at the same school?

"Don't worry about Ben," Sam sneered. "All the teachers think he's a genius – the little nerd."

Sam managed to keep his head down for a while, but then he was suspended for a week and the Head Teacher said that he would be expelled if anything else happened.

That's when Dad stepped in. He came round and had a long talk with Mum and they decided that Sam would go and live with him full time.

When Sam went out of the door with Dad he gave me a big grin and a thumbs-up. And I realised – he had done it all on purpose. It had taken a long time but he had got what he wanted – he was going to live with Dad.

"I know Sam can be a pain a lot of the time," Mum said that evening. "But when he's nice, it's like the sun coming out from behind a cloud."

I knew what she meant. But the sunshine didn't make up for the rest.

Chapter 4
The First Dare

When Sam went to live with Dad he was supposed
to spend weekends with Mum, but most times
he had a match or training so he didn't show up.
But I still had to go to Dad's every weekend.

Every week I tried to think of things I could
do or say to please Dad, but as soon as I got to his
place I felt all clumsy and awkward. I dropped
things or knocked things over. I couldn't think of
anything interesting to say so I kept my mouth
shut.

"What's up with you?" Dad would say. "Are
you in a mood?"

All I could do was shake my head or give a
silly laugh.

I even tried to get into the junior rugby team again to prove I wasn't a coward, but I never got picked. So I decided to show Dad how good I was at swimming instead. One Saturday morning I plucked up the nerve to say, "Hey, Dad – can we go to the pool this afternoon?"

"You know I can't stand all that splashing about, Ben," he said. "I'll drive you there if you want but I won't come in. Anyway, Sam's got a big match this afternoon and I thought we could go and watch."

It was even worse the few times Sam spent the weekend with Mum and I was alone with Dad. He kept saying things like, "I wonder what Sam's up to?" The hours dragged by and I couldn't wait to go home.

But Mum loved those weekends with Sam. She always told me how nice he had been and how he had changed for the better.

I could have told her the truth, but I didn't.

The truth was that Sam was worse. Much worse. He was always in trouble at school and at weekends he hung out with some older lads in the rugby club. They were all heavy drinkers and

Sam would often stagger home blind drunk at all hours.

The first time Sam dared me to do something was with those lads at the rugby club.

Dad was in a side room for a meeting and Sam and his mates were in the bar. They were drunk and were singing dirty songs round the old piano. I was in a corner, playing a game on my phone and trying to be invisible.

One of the songs was really filthy, but it was super funny and it made me laugh out loud. Sam heard me. "Hey, Chick, come and sing with us," he shouted.

"I don't want to," I said, but Sam grabbed my arm and dragged me over to the piano.

"You need a drink to get you going," he said. "Come on, guys. Let's mix up something for my little brother – get him in the mood."

They got a pint glass and they all tipped a bit of their drink in it – beer and cider and vodka and whisky.

"Come on, Chick," Sam said, and he held out the glass.

I shook my head.

Sam came close and whispered in my ear. "Don't let me down," he said. "I don't want my mates to think I've got a wimp for a brother. Come on, I dare you."

He shoved the glass in my hand.

"Down in one," he said and began to stamp his feet.

All his mates joined in, stamping and shouting. "Drink, drink!"

I raised the glass. The smell was awful, but I gulped and gulped until it was all gone.

There was a huge cheer as I finished it.

Sam put his arm round me. "Yeah – you did it!" he said. "I'm proud of you, Chick."

The taste in my mouth was foul but I didn't care. Sam was proud of me. He and his friends started to sing again and I joined in. Sam was right – it was easy to let go and have a good time with a drink inside you. I sang as loud as I could and half way into the song the rest of them stopped singing but I went on.

"Hey, great little singer!" someone yelled at the end.

They started the song again and I joined in, louder than ever. But all of a sudden I began to laugh and I couldn't stop. The song was so filthy and so funny. I laughed and laughed. Then the room began to spin and I felt hot and sweaty. A sour taste of puke rose up in my throat.

I fixed my eyes on the door and started to walk over to it. I could feel myself swaying from side to side and it seemed to take ages to cross the floor. At last, I reached the door and went outside. The cold air hit me and cleared my head. I was going to be OK. But I wanted to sit down.

I walked over to Dad's car and tried the door. It was unlocked so I got in. As soon as I sat down another wave of sickness hit me. I fell to the side and threw up.

The next thing I knew, Dad was shaking me. I sat up and saw the sick all over me and on the seat. The smell was vile and I threw up again.

"Look at the state of you! Look at my car!" Dad shouted. "You stupid little git!"

The next morning I still felt ill. My head throbbed and the smell of breakfast made me heave.

"Serves you right," Dad said. "Now get out there and clean my car. I want it looking and smelling like new."

It took me nearly two hours to clean the inside of the car and then Dad made me wash my clothes by hand.

That almost made me sick again, but in the end I got all the stains out.

I spent the rest of the day in bed. I still had the taste of booze and puke in my mouth and I told myself I would never drink again.

Dad didn't even say goodbye when it was time for me to go home. But as I opened the front door to leave, Sam grabbed hold of me.

"You're not such a wimp after all," he said. "Nice one, bro. We'll have more of the same next weekend, eh?"

Chapter 5
Job Done

"Nice one, bro!"

I clung on to those words as if they were proof that Sam loved me. And I remembered them any time he was nasty, which was most of the time. And then, on top of everything, he got into trouble with the police.

The first time was on Sam's 17th birthday. He went into town with his mates and got very drunk. On the way home he started chatting up some girl outside a chip shop. When her boyfriend came out, he pushed Sam away and Sam pushed back. Next thing, there was a full-on fight. They punched and kicked each other, then Sam chucked a bottle. It missed the guy but broke a shop window.

Just then a cop car turned up. The other guy ran away, but the cops got hold of Sam. They rang Dad, who promised them he would deal with Sam. When Sam got home he had a black eye, a cut lip and blood dripping from his nose. Dad shouted at him, but Sam was so drunk he just slumped on the kitchen floor and fell asleep.

The second time, Sam was in a stolen car that crashed into a tree. The other two guys in the car were taken to hospital, but Sam didn't have a scratch on him. Sam hadn't stolen the car and he wasn't driving, but the police took him to the station to question him and Dad had to go to pick him up.

"That's it, you're grounded for a month," Dad told Sam.

Sam grinned and put his arm round Dad. "Come on, Dad," he said. "It's not like I'm a serial killer. I was unlucky. It was just wrong place, wrong time." Then he added in a silly voice, "Forgive me?"

Dad tried to look serious but he couldn't hide the little smile on his face. No matter what Sam did, no matter what problems he caused them,

Mum and Dad could never stay angry at him for long.

And me – I just wanted him to like me. I hated it when he teased me or bullied me, but I hated it even more when he ignored me. I wanted to please him. I couldn't be the sporty brother he wanted so I tried to find other ways to make him happy.

I stored up every joke I heard – especially the dirty ones – so I could make him laugh. I watched all his cricket and rugby games and told him how good he was.

And I gave him money. He was always broke and asking me for a loan. I didn't have much but I gave him what I had.

"Pay you back next week, Chick," Sam always said. But he never did.

And then there were the dares.

I suppose part of me liked it when he dared me to do something because it meant he was taking notice of me. And I did them, no matter how stupid or wrong or dangerous they were. I ran across busy roads in front of speeding cars because Sam dared me. I nicked money from

Dad's wallet or Mum's purse and gave it to Sam because he dared me to.

One time Sam dared me to climb out of our bedroom window in the block of flats where Dad lived and walk along the ledge to the living room. Dad's flat was three floors up, and the ledge was only about 20 centimetres wide, but I couldn't say no.

I climbed out onto the ledge and pressed my face against the wall so I wouldn't have to look down. I shuffled along, terrified that my feet would slip. Then, when I got to the living-room window, Sam laughed at me and wouldn't let me in and I had to shuffle all the way back to the bedroom window. I really thought I was going to wet myself. By the time I got back inside, my legs were trembling.

Another time Sam dared me to pierce my ear with a needle. It hurt like hell but I did it. The hole in my ear got infected and yellow pus oozed out of it, so I had to see the doctor.

Mum was furious. "What the hell did you do that for?" she said. Of course, I didn't tell her.

All Sam ever said when I did his dares was, "Job done." But those two words always put a smile on my face.

It was crazy really. I got praise from Mum all the time for my school reports and my drawings and paintings. My exam forecasts were all good. I was in the school swimming team and my music teacher said I was her best pupil.

But I would have swapped it all just to be good at rugby or cricket or football. The only praise I really wanted was praise from Dad and Sam.

And Sam most of all.

Chapter 6
Graffiti

At the end of the summer term the school put on a talent show. My music teacher made me play my guitar and sing. She chose an old song called 'You Stand By Me'. I tried to jazz it up but I thought it still sounded lame, so I was amazed when I won.

The next day in Assembly the Head Teacher, Mrs Baxter, gave me my prize in front of the whole school and then asked me to sing the song again. The applause at the end was brilliant – even louder than at the talent show – and I was buzzing all morning. Until I met Sam in the playground at break.

"You looked a right prat up there, Chick," he said.

"So?"

"So, you think you're cool cos you won some crap singing prize!"

"What about you?" I said. "You were dead chuffed when you got that cup for being rugby captain."

"That's different," Sam said. "That's sport. And I don't go around sucking up to the teachers, like you. 'Thank you, Mrs Baxter! Let me kiss your bum, Mrs Baxter! Ooh, let me sing a crap song, Mrs Baxter!'"

"I didn't choose that song," I snapped. "And I don't suck up to teachers."

"Yeah? Well prove it. I dare you to ..." Sam thought for a minute then said, "I dare you to spray a tag or some graffiti on the wall tonight."

"Like what?" I asked.

There was no way I was going to write some of the stuff Sam came out with, but in the end I agreed to spray-paint BAXTER IS GAGGING 4 IT on the wall. I knew it was stupid, but Sam thought it was funny and I wanted to please him.

And so at 10 o'clock that night I climbed over the fence into the playground and spray-painted those stupid words. When I got home I saw that I'd got paint all over my hands and I spent ages trying to wash it off. But there was still some on my fingers when I went to school the next morning.

I walked into the playground and saw the caretaker scrubbing the words off the wall. It was still obvious what it said and loads of kids were watching and laughing. All day long people talked about it and when I saw Sam in the corridor he said, "Job done, Chick."

Then he pointed to the red paint on my fingers. "Better hide that," he said. "They're gonna come round and check everyone's hands!"

For the rest of the day I nearly passed out with fear when anyone opened the classroom door in case it was a teacher come to check our hands.

After school I told Sam he was wrong – there hadn't been any checks. He laughed. "Joke, duh!" he said.

Chapter 7
Showing Off

Sam got a girlfriend in the summer holidays.
She was called Holly and he was crazy about her.
I didn't like her much but I had to admit she had
beautiful green eyes and a gorgeous smile. The
best thing was that Sam spent so much time with
Holly that he didn't have time to pick on me.
Except one afternoon when she came round to
Dad's flat.

"Get lost, Chick – we want some privacy,"
Sam said.

I got up and headed towards our bedroom.

"Not there, thicko!" Sam said. "Out! Right
outside. Go and play in the traffic or something."

Holly giggled.

"Why should I?" I said.

"Because I tell you to," Sam said, and he pushed me over to the front door. "You've been in my way ever since you were born. Now get out and stay out!"

From then on, I had to go out every time Holly came round, but at least it kept Sam off my back. All Sam could think about was Holly, Holly, Holly, and he did everything he could to impress her. As soon as the sun came out he took his shirt off so she could admire his muscles and his six-pack. He showed her the cups he'd won for rugby and the photos of him playing. He even got her to come to watch a cricket match, but she said it was about as much fun as having your teeth pulled out. Sam never asked her again.

The summer sped by and soon we were back at school. It was Sam's last year and he had important exams coming up. He even started to work a bit, but he was so far behind he had to ask me about the basics. I was happy to help, but he was a useless student and he got angry with me when he didn't understand things.

The music teacher decided to put on a musical and asked me to be in it. I only agreed because it meant I got to play my electric guitar for a couple of the songs, but she soon got me to sing and dance too. I liked the singing but I found the dancing really hard. It was like when I tried to play football – my feet kept getting in a muddle. It took me ages to learn the steps that other people found easy.

I was dead nervous, but the first night of the show went really well and everyone told me how good I was – even my dancing. Mum loved it, of course. And Dad came, too, and said it was OK.

Sam didn't agree with them. The next day he poked me in the chest. "What's up with you, always showing off?" he asked.

"I'm not!" I said.

"That's what it looked like, prancing around on stage like a gayboy."

I went red. "The rest of the school thought it was good."

"Well, I didn't," Sam jeered. "I always thought you were gay."

"I'm not!" I walked away.

For the next couple of weeks Sam whispered "gayboy" every time I saw him at school. I pretended that I didn't care but inside I began to worry. *Was* I gay? And would it matter if I was? Lots of other people were. But how did you know if you were? I wasn't good at rugby and football – maybe that was a sign.

I remembered all the times I'd sneaked a look at other lads in the showers. But everyone did that, didn't they? Just checking you were the same. It wasn't like I fancied them or anything.

I fancied girls, but I'd never had a girlfriend and all my friends were boys. I told myself that didn't mean anything – most boys hung around with other boys, even the ones who boasted about what they'd done with girls. I thought and thought about it and I was pretty sure I wasn't gay. But I was never 100% sure – especially when Sam called me "gayboy".

Chapter 8

Loser

I'd been doing life-saving classes all term and in the last week before the Christmas holiday, we had exams for our bronze awards. We all did the theory questions together, then I was first to do the practical tests in the school swimming pool. At the end of my test they told me that I'd passed and I could go and get dressed.

As I came out of the changing room I found Sam and his friend, Jake, in the corridor. They were looking in the window and laughing at one of the girls who was waiting on the side of the pool to do her test.

"Look at the rack on Lyla!" Sam said to me when I stopped next to him.

"I bet she's hot at the *breast* stroke!" Jake said. "That rack must help her float!"

Lyla was in my class and I really liked her, but I wanted to please Sam so I laughed. "Yeah," I said. "Think how big her bra must be!"

Bad mistake.

Sam looked at me and a wicked grin lit up his face. "Let's find out!" he said. "Come on."

Sam and Jake dragged me along the corridor to the girls' changing room.

"OK, Chick – go in there, find her bra and bring it out to show us," Sam said.

"Oh come on, Sam," I said. "No way!"

"Don't be chicken," he said. "I dare you!"

Jake opened the door and Sam pushed me inside. The door slammed shut. I tried to open it, but Sam and Jake were holding it from the other side. I was lucky – the changing room was empty. But one of the girls might come in at any moment.

"Let me out," I shouted.

"Only if you find the bra," Sam called.

I stopped pulling on the door and ran along the rows of pegs, looking for Lyla's clothes. Why had I opened my stupid mouth? I had no idea how big her bra was. How would I know if it was hers or not? Maybe I could just grab any bra – Sam wouldn't know.

I was just about to do that when I saw an open sports bag with the name 'Lyla White' written on the inside. I looked at the clothes on the peg above it. Sweater. Skirt. Blouse. Knickers. I felt like some kind of pervert, going through her clothes.

Where was the bra? Where was it? Not on the peg. It must be in the sports bag.

And there it was. Maybe Lyla really had hidden it, because it was enormous.

I ran to the door and banged on it. "I've got it!" I shouted.

The door opened and I stepped into the corridor.

"Here it is! It's like a tent," I laughed, and I held it up in front of me.

There was a flash and I saw Jake with his phone.

"No, Jake – delete that photo!" I said and tried to grab the phone off him, but he and Sam ran off down the corridor.

I ducked back into the changing room with the bra. By the time I got to Lyla's peg, I could hear girls' voices. They were in the showers. Any minute they would finish and come round the corner and see me.

I panicked and dropped the bra. It fell onto the floor but there was no time to pick it up. I dived for the door and got through it just as the girls came into the changing room. I ran down the corridor and out into the playground. I was safe.

Or so I thought.

That evening I was playing a game on my phone when I got a text from Sam. "Hey check out 'bra-boy' on Twitter. You're trending!"

I went onto Twitter and typed in '#bra-boy'. There was Jake's photo of me, with the bra in front of my chest. Under it, it said, "I want to be a girl."

There were masses of comments under the photo – all rude. And I saw that the photo had been shared on all the sites I knew my mates looked at.

The next day at school was hell. Everyone had seen the photo. People kept making comments and calling me "bra-boy".

Just after lunch Mrs Baxter sent for me. Someone had shown her the Twitter photo and she knew it had been taken in the school. She asked me where I'd got the bra and I lied and said I'd found it in the corridor. Of course Mrs Baxter didn't believe me, but I stuck to the story. She threatened to write to Mum and Dad. I begged her not to and I promised I'd never do anything like it again.

"You're lucky your school work is so good and that you haven't been in trouble before – as far as I know," Mrs Baxter said. She gave me an intense look as if she was trying to find out anything else I'd done. I blushed as I thought about the stupid graffiti on the wall. "This is a final warning, Ben," Mrs Baxter said. "Grow up a bit, please. Now get out of here."

But the worst thing of all happened when I was leaving school. Lyla was waiting outside the gate.

"It was my bra, wasn't it, in that photo?" she said.

I couldn't lie to her. I nodded, feeling stupid and embarrassed.

"I used to think you were OK, but you're just a loser," she said.

She walked away and joined a group of friends who were waiting for her. They laughed as they went off down the street and I knew they were laughing at me.

I felt like a stupid little kid. Ben the loser.

It was all Sam's fault.

"Never again," I told myself. "I'll never let Sam make me do a dare again."

Chapter 9
Love in the Air

I went shopping a few days before Christmas. I was standing at the bus stop waiting to go home when someone tapped me on the arm. It was Sam.

"Hey Chick!" He was smiling and he seemed glad to see me. "Want to get something to eat? I could murder a burger. Come on, bro."

I said yes at once. We crossed the road and went into McDonald's. When we got to the counter I only ordered a shake, but Sam ordered a double cheeseburger, large fries and a Coke. The girl asked for our money and Sam turned to me.

"I'm broke, Chick – can you get this?"

I only had just enough money and it would mean I would have to walk home, but I didn't care. I paid and we went to a table.

I sipped my shake while Sam wolfed down his food.

"Mmm, tasty!" he said, then he did a loud burp. "Cheers, Chick, you're a mate."

I grinned, glad to be Sam's mate again.

"You been shopping?" he asked.

I nodded.

"I did mine yesterday," Sam said. "Got 'em all except Holly's. The problem is I'm skint. Can you do me a big favour, Chick?"

"What?"

"I know what she'd really like – a bottle of Love in the Air. It's her favourite perfume. But it costs a fortune."

"I haven't got any money, Sam."

"I don't want money." He stopped and looked at me and I knew he was going to get me into trouble. "They've got the perfume in that big store across the road. Can you go and nick a bottle for me?"

"No!" I said. "If you want it so much, why don't you nick it yourself?"

Sam scowled. "Cos I've got a police record after that stupid car accident, that's why."

"Yeah, well I don't want to get a police record, thanks," I told him.

"You won't," he said. "Look at you – you look like a little angel. No one's gonna suspect you."

"Get stuffed!"

"Go on, Chick – do it for me."

"No."

"Chick, come on. It'll be easy. I dare you."

Those three terrible words. "I dare you."

They were like some kind of spell that scrambled my brain.

I knew it was crazy. And I'd promised myself I'd never do one of his dares again. But I wanted to carry on being Sam's mate.

"OK," I said at last.

Chapter 10

Six Seconds

The store was very hot and crowded. Jolly Christmas music was playing but nobody looked happy. They pushed and shoved each other as they went from one department to another.

I was pleased it was so busy. Maybe no one would notice me in the middle of the crowd.

I checked the signs and saw that the Perfume department was off to the right. To get there I had to make my way past all the displays of women's clothes.

As I passed the underwear I remembered all the trouble from Sam's last dare. And I knew that if this one went wrong the fall-out would be worse. Much worse.

I forced my way through the shoppers buying watches and jewellery and came to the Perfume counters.

I walked up and down the aisles as if I didn't know what I wanted to buy. But all the time I kept my eyes open to see if there were any store detectives around. The trouble was I knew they made themselves look like ordinary shoppers so that it was difficult to tell who they were. Was that woman over there staring at me? And were hidden CCTV cameras pointed at me right now?

My heart beat fast and sweat trickled down my sides. The heat from the shop and the sweet smell of all the perfume was making me feel dizzy.

Where were the bottles of Love in the Air? I walked along the displays again but I couldn't see them. Perhaps they had sold out. For a moment, I was pleased – I wouldn't have to do Sam's dare. Then I turned and saw a stack of them on a glass counter next to the till.

I would never be able to steal a bottle from there. A sales woman was standing right next to the display. I wanted to go out and tell Sam it was impossible, but he would think I had let him down. And I didn't want to do that. I wanted to be his mate.

Then a woman went to the counter and asked if she could try a perfume before she bought it. The sales woman turned and went to get a tester bottle from the back shelf. I counted how long it took her. She had her back turned for six seconds. That would give me time if I was fast.

The woman decided she didn't like the perfume and went away.

Easy.

I walked over to the perfume counter.

"Can I help?" the sales woman said.

"Can I smell a perfume?" I asked.

"Of course," the sales woman said. "Which one?"

I panicked. I didn't know the names of any perfumes except Love in the Air. I didn't want to ask for that in case the tester was on the counter.

"It's for my mum," I said. "She likes flowers. Roses."

The sales woman thought for a moment then turned away to get a tester.

Six seconds. I had six seconds to do it.

One. Two … I took a box of Love in the Air from the counter and dropped it into my bag of presents.

"This is one of our most popular perfumes," the sales woman said as she came back towards me with a bottle. "See what you think."

She squirted some perfume onto a piece of card and held it out for me to smell. I bent my head and sniffed.

"It's nice," I said. "But I'm not sure. I'll come back tomorrow."

I wanted to run out of there as fast as I could but I forced myself to walk normally. Past the jewellery. Past the clothes. The crowds of shoppers blocked my way and slowed me down. My heart was thudding in my chest. But there, at last, was the exit.

I pushed open the doors and stepped out onto the pavement.

I saw Sam across the road. He put his thumb up and smiled when he saw me. Then the smile faded and he shouted something. One word. I couldn't hear because of the traffic. But it looked like – "Run!"

Then a big hand grabbed my arm and turned me round.

"I think you'd better come with me," the man said.

Chapter 11
I Just Don't Get You

The store detective led me back into the shop.

The manager's office was at the back of the building on the second floor and that was where the store detective took me. He had my arm in a firm grip and people turned and looked as we went past. I burned with shame. It was obvious that I was a thief who had been caught.

The manager was on the phone when we got to his office. I stood in front of his desk and waited. He went on and on talking. Five minutes. Seven minutes. Ten minutes went by and I got more and more scared.

"Well, what have we got here?" the manager said when at last he put the phone down.

The detective tipped my bag onto the desk and the box of Love in the Air tumbled out with my presents.

"All this?" the manager asked.

"I only saw him take the perfume," the detective said.

"They're presents – I've paid for them," I said and pointed to the receipts among the packages.

The manager sorted through the receipts. "And where's the one for this perfume?" he said.

I hung my head.

"Right," he said, and he picked up a pen. "Name and address?"

I told him.

"Age?"

"14," I said.

"We have a policy in this store – we always prosecute shoplifters," the manager said. "A nice Christmas present for your parents when the police go round to see them. And, of course, your school will be informed."

A wave of heat spread up my body to my face and I felt as if I was going to faint.

"Please – don't," I said.

There was a knock and the manager looked up as the door opened.

"Is my brother here?" a voice said.

It was Sam.

He walked over to me and put his arm round me. "Right, what's going on here?" he said.

The manager began to explain, but Sam interrupted him. "Let's get one thing clear," he said. "This boy is under age. It's against the law to question him without an adult present. I've phoned our father and he should be here in a couple of minutes."

The manager sat there with his mouth open for a moment, then he said he would wait for our dad. Sam and I sat on some chairs near the door and waited. Sam winked at me but I was worried. What would Dad do when he arrived? Would he be angry? Would he shout at me?

But all that happened was he came in, nodded at me and Sam, then grilled the manager. The detective told the story all over again.

"This is what he stole, is it?" Dad asked, and he held up the box of perfume.

"That's correct," the manager said.

"How much does it cost? I'll pay for it," Dad said.

The manager shook his head. "I'm afraid that's not the point. The boy was caught stealing and we always prosecute shoplifters."

"So, you would rather prosecute a young boy than accept payment?" Dad said. "I can't wait to tell that to the editor of the local paper. He's a friend of mine."

The manager blinked and I could see that he was thinking about the bad publicity.

"Wait a minute," Dad said, and he held up the perfume box again. "This says 'Display only'. What does that mean?"

Before anyone could reply, Dad opened the box. He looked inside and then tipped it upside down. Strips of cardboard fell out. When they stopped falling he looked inside again, then smiled at the manager. "Oops – no perfume. Now, is it your policy to prosecute my son for stealing bits of cardboard? Well, is it?"

The manager blinked again. Then he shook his head.

"Good," Dad said. "Sam, Ben – we're going."

We followed him out of the room, down the stairs and out onto the pavement. Nobody spoke as we walked to the car park. Then, when we got to the car, Dad turned and pushed me up against the door.

"What the bloody hell were you playing at, stealing a bottle of perfume?"

I could see Sam behind him. He shook his head, begging me not to tell the truth.

"I don't know," I said.

"You don't know? What kind of answer is that?" Dad shouted. "What are you, an idiot? I just don't get you."

There was anger and disappointment in his eyes and he turned away as if he couldn't bear to look at me.

We got in the car and started to drive home.

There was a terrible silence until Sam said, "Is the editor of the local newspaper really one of your friends?"

"Never met him in my life!" Dad said.

"You crafty liar," Sam said and they both burst into laughter.

That was Sam – he could make Dad laugh.

All I could do was disappoint him.

Chapter 12
The Storm

As soon as we got back to Dad's flat he rang Mum and told her what had happened. When I went home the next day she was even angrier than Dad had been. Worse than that, she cried. I'd never done anything to make her cry before.

"It was only a display box with cardboard in it," I said.

"That's not the point," she said. "You stole it. I just don't understand why. Why?"

I couldn't tell her and she started crying again. I tried to comfort her, but she pushed me away and didn't talk to me all day even though it was Christmas Eve.

Sam came round to Mum's on Christmas Day. We opened presents and Mum was pleased with the bracelet I'd got her.

"And he didn't nick it!" Sam joked.

Mum didn't laugh and I could have kicked him.

I went round to Dad's on Boxing Day. I had got a pen for Dad and Sam made the same joke.

"I'd be down on you like a ton of bricks if I found out this was nicked," Dad said, and he waved the pen at me.

He wasn't joking. Worse still, I knew he didn't really like the pen. He was much more pleased with the rugby DVD box set Sam had got him.

Sam went out in the afternoon to see Holly and I watched two football matches on TV with Dad. He was really into the games so I pretended to be interested, too. He gave me a bottle of beer. I didn't like the taste, but it felt good to sit next to him and drink a beer together.

When Sam came home in the evening I went into the bedroom for a chat.

"Did you give Holly a present?" I asked.

"Yeah, a rubbish box of chocolates instead of her favourite perfume," Sam said. Then he laughed. "You are totally a crap thief, Chick!"

"That's me!" I said. "Thanks for coming to get me, though. I reckon they would have called the police if you hadn't turned up."

"What else could I do, mate?" Sam said. "You're my bro. Blood's thicker than water, innit? Anyway, it all worked out in the end."

"Yeah, except I made Mum cry and Dad thinks I'm an idiot."

"Course he doesn't," Sam said.

"He does – he said so. Plus he still thinks I'm a coward."

I was hoping Sam would tell me it wasn't true, but of course he didn't.

"Well, you are chicken, admit it," he said. "Plus you're into all that gayboy singing and music stuff. Being a swot. Reading books. When did you ever see Dad with a book? He just thinks you're a bit ... weird. But he still loves you – don't ask me why."

We went into the living room and Sam sat next to Dad on the sofa. They didn't leave space for me, so I sat on another chair. And Dad offered Sam a beer.

"You're not having another one," Dad said to me. "Don't want you puking all over the furniture!"

Sam laughed and switched on the TV. He flicked up and down the channels and found a horror film.

Sam and Dad loved scary films but stuff like that freaked me out. I stuck it out for about half an hour but I knew I'd have bad dreams if I watched any more.

I yawned and said, "I'm knackered. Think I'll go to bed."

But I couldn't fool Sam. As I reached the door he shouted out, "Baby's scared he's gonna mess his nappy! Chick-Chick-Chicken!"

And Dad laughed.

I went to my bedroom and wished I was at home with Mum, but she had gone up north to visit an old friend. She'd be gone for three days.

Three days with Sam and Dad. Three whole days of them calling me chicken.

I got undressed and got into bed. I turned off the light and tried not to think about that film – it had been really creepy.

I was just drifting off to sleep when a tapping sound jolted me awake. A shiver ran through me until I realised it was only rain being blown against the window. A moment later there was a flash of lightning and a crack of thunder that shook the building.

I couldn't help it. I pulled the covers up over my head. Sam and Dad were right. I was a wimp. A chicken.

But if I'd known what would happen because of that storm, I would have been even more scared.

Chapter 13

Three Terrible Words

It seemed as if the rain would never stop. It poured all the next day and the day after, too.

Dad was out at work and Sam didn't get up until late, so I spent a lot of time reading.

"You geeky little bookworm," Sam snarled at me when at last he got up.

Of course it was different when he asked me to read a book to help him revise for his exams.

All the revision made Sam very bad tempered. He acted as if it was my fault if he didn't understand something. And when he forgot what I'd tried to teach him he swore and went into a sulk.

"It's all right for you, you bloody swot," he'd say when he got another answer wrong.

So I was glad on the third day when he decided to skip revision and go round to Holly's.

He was only gone for about an hour. I don't know if he had a row with Holly or what, but he was in a weird mood when he came back. He was soaking wet, but he didn't change his clothes or dry his hair or anything. He didn't say a word, just looked at me with a funny kind of smile on his face, then went and stared out of the window.

"Do you want to do some revision?" I asked him.

"I've got a better idea," he said and walked into our bedroom. He came back with his camera. "Come on, Chick – we're going out."

"Where?"

"You know that little river the other side of the park? It's flooded. It looks awesome. I want to take some photos. Come on, it'll be ace."

I should have said no. I could see that strange little smile round his lips and I should have known he had a plan. Sam's plans were always bad news. But I wanted to do something with him, like brothers do. So I said OK.

It was still pouring with rain when we got to the river. Sam was right – it looked awesome. It was so high that if there was much more rain it would burst the banks. We stood on the new bridge and watched the water as it raced below us.

"Look, the pillars are almost underwater," Sam said.

He pointed to the seven concrete pillars that stretched from one bank to the other. They had formed the base of the old wooden bridge that had gone rotten and been torn down a couple of years ago. Usually the tops of the pillars stood about a metre above the river, but now the water swirled and splashed over them.

"Hey, I've got an idea," Sam said.

My tummy flipped. This was it.

"I reckon you could jump from the bank onto the first pillar. And then skip from one to the other all the way to the other side. That would be a laugh."

"Ha ha. I don't think so," I said.

"It'd be easy," Sam went on. "How far apart are the pillars? A metre, max? Simple."

"Oh yeah. Go on then," I said.

"Not me – you."

"No way."

"Come on, Chick. You always say Dad thinks you're a coward. Well, prove you're not. I'll film you on my camera. We can show him tonight."

I shook my head. "No way, Sam."

But Sam didn't give up. "Look, Dad thinks you're a wimp, right?" he said. "So prove you're not by doing something."

"Something dangerous! Yeah, right! I could get killed."

"It's not dangerous. But I'll go over to the other bank and film it so it looks more dangerous than it is. Dad will be well impressed."

"No way, Sam."

And then he said it – those three terrible words.

"I dare you."

Chapter 14

The Raging River

I stood on the bank and looked across the swollen river. The water roared past, wild and fast and dangerous. Sam stood on the other side with his camera. Waiting.

I looked at the gap from the bank to the first pillar. I leaned forward and stretched out my leg. It was too wide to step. I would have to jump. A little wave swept over the top of the pillar. It would be slippery now.

"Come on, Chick," Sam shouted. "I've started to film. One. Two. Three. Go!"

I took a deep breath and jumped.

My feet splashed down in the middle of the pillar. I wobbled a bit as I landed but I put my arms out and got my balance.

"Great!" Sam shouted. "That was the hard bit. Now skip across to me."

I looked at the six pillars that stretched ahead of me. It was true that they weren't as far apart as the first one. Maybe Sam was right and I would be able skip my way across. I swung my leg and jumped. I landed on the second pillar and, without stopping, I sprang forward and leaped onto the third, then onto the fourth.

As I hit the fourth pillar, my foot slipped and I almost skidded off into the water. I slammed my back foot down and stopped the slide.

"Bloody hell!" I shouted. It had been a close thing. My heart was pounding.

Sam was shouting, "Jump! Jump!" But I couldn't do it. All my confidence had gone. I waited a bit then stretched my leg out and stepped onto the fifth pillar and waited again. Then onto the sixth, then onto the seventh and at last I jumped onto the bank next to Sam.

"That was rubbish, Chick," Sam said as he stopped filming. "It was great at the start. Then the last bit was crap."

"I almost fell!"

"You wouldn't have fallen if you'd kept going," he said. "You just have to get into the rhythm of it. Here, take my camera – I'll show you."

"No, Sam – don't," I said. "Those pillars are really slippery. If you go too fast you'll fall."

"Fall? Me? No way! Watch and learn from the master!" Sam shoved the camera into my hands and moved to the edge of the bank.

He took one step back, swayed, then jumped from the bank onto the first pillar.

"Sam!" I shouted. "Be careful in the middle."

But Sam was off. He skipped from pillar to pillar all the way across. He looked so graceful and I could see what he meant about getting into the rhythm. He made it look so easy.

He jumped onto the far bank and turned round with a big grin on his face. "Whoooooo!" he shouted, and he pumped his arms in the air. "Who's the daddy?"

"You are!" I yelled back.

"Here I come," he shouted, and he moved forward to the edge of the bank.

"No, Sam – use the bridge!"

"Nah!" he jeered. "The bridge is for wimps! Watch me."

And he set off again across the river.

Almost at once, I could see what was going to happen.

His rhythm was wrong. He was moving too fast. He was jumping too high.

He hit the fourth pillar. His front foot skidded and flew up into the air.

He slid off the pillar and crashed backwards.

I saw the back of his head hit the concrete. I heard the crack of his skull over the roar of the raging river.

Then Sam tumbled into the water and was swept away by the current.

Chapter 15
Don't Die

I ran along the side of the river, trying to keep up with Sam as the water swirled him downstream.

Out of the corner of my eye I saw a car coming up the road on the top of the bank. I scrambled half way up the bank and shouted and waved my arms. The car jerked to a stop. The driver wound down his window.

"My brother's fallen in the river," I screamed.

"I'll phone for help," the guy shouted.

I ran back down the slope. Sam was a long way downstream now. I tore after him and little by little I got closer. To my horror, I saw that he had rolled over and was floating face down. If I didn't do something fast he would drown.

I ran past him, kicked off my trainers and then jumped into the river and swam out to the middle of the stream. The current was strong and it pulled me along with it, turning me around and around.

Sam went past before I could get to him and I thrashed my arms and legs to try to catch up with him.

I gasped for air and swallowed some water. I coughed and spluttered but I had to keep on swimming, following Sam.

Twice I got near and reached out to catch him. But twice my hand splashed down into the water behind him.

The river began to bend to the right and the stream pulled us both in towards the left bank. Then the current twisted us round and out towards the centre again.

We were moving faster now. I knew why. We were near the weir. If we went much further we would crash over the top and fall two metres down the concrete drop on the other side. The churning water at the bottom would trap us and drown us both.

My body felt weaker and weaker and my clothes were dragging me down but I swam as hard as I could, closer and closer to Sam.

The current spun him round and I reached out and grabbed his arm.

I pulled and his head came up out of the water. I dragged him close and slipped my hands under his arms and round his chest.

I lay back in the water with him and I kicked my legs.

Slowly, oh so slowly, we moved away from the middle of the stream and headed towards the bank. It was all I could do to support Sam and stop myself sinking under his weight. I could hear the roar of the water as it poured over the weir.

We were being spun round and round but somehow I kept kicking and the river bank got closer.

There was a branch hanging down from a tree and I let go of Sam with one hand and grabbed hold of it. We jerked to a stop and Sam swung round with me. We were next to the bank, but there was no way I could lift him out without letting go of the branch.

The cold of the water was beginning to numb my whole body. Sam's face was close to mine and I could see that he was pale and his lips were blue. His blood poured out of the wound on his head and onto me.

My arm began to tremble. I wouldn't be able to hold the branch much longer. We would be swept away again and over the weir.

"Take my hand!"

I looked up – it was the young guy from the car. He was on his knees on the bank, holding out his hand. I grabbed it.

He pulled me and at the same time I pushed Sam onto the bank. The river was so high that we were level with the top of the bank and the guy got hold of Sam and rolled him onto dry land.

Sam was lying on his front and, as soon as I climbed out of the water, I turned him over.

I put my face close to his nose and mouth.

He wasn't breathing.

I felt for a pulse in his neck.

Nothing.

For a moment I panicked, and then I forced myself to remember everything I'd learned in life-saving.

I opened Sam's mouth, pinched his nose and breathed into him five times. Then I began pumping his chest.

"The police and ambulance are on their way," the guy said.

I kept pumping my brother's chest and giving him the kiss of life. Over and over and over.

All I could think was, "Don't die, Sam. Don't die."

And I pumped his chest and breathed my breath into him until I felt strong hands pull me off.

It was a man in uniform.

The police and the paramedics were there and they took over.

"Is he dead?" I kept saying.

But someone put a blanket round my shoulders and led me away to an ambulance.

Chapter 16
Too Shocked to Speak

As I got into the ambulance the young guy from the car ran up and handed me Sam's camera.

Then the ambulance doors closed and we set off.

"What about my brother?" I said.

"He'll be right behind us," the paramedic said.

"Will he be all right?"

"I'm sure they're doing their best," the paramedic said.

What did that mean? Was he trying to tell me that Sam was dead? I didn't dare ask.

I didn't ask when we got to the hospital. I didn't ask when they did all kinds of tests on me in A&E. I didn't ask when they put me in a bed in a side room. I didn't ask when they brought me a hot chocolate and made me drink it even though I didn't want to.

If I didn't ask, it would mean Sam was alive.

Nurses came and went, but I just lay there and the minutes ticked by.

"Ben."

I looked up and Dad was there. He sat on the bed and pulled me into a hug.

"Thank God you're OK," he said, and he stroked the top of my head.

I could feel tears in my eyes so I pressed myself against his chest so that he wouldn't see them.

And there, holding on to him, I had to ask.

"Is Sam all right, Dad?"

Dad let go of me and I saw his pale face and his worried eyes.

"They're operating on him. It's very serious – but they're doing everything they can." Dad's voice cracked and he pulled me into a hug again.

I could hear his heart thudding. "The police told me what you did. Oh Ben! If it hadn't been for you, Sam would be dead. You were so brave. So brave. You saved him!"

He started to sob. I'd never seen him cry and now my tears began to fall, too.

We stayed there for a long time, hugging each other and crying. Then a doctor came. She examined me and said that I was OK to get up. Dad had brought some dry clothes for me and I got dressed, then we went to the waiting room.

Hours went by. We sat. Not talking. Just holding hands. Waiting.

I fell asleep with my head in Dad's lap.

I could hear Mum's voice and I thought I was dreaming, but when I opened my eyes she was there. She cried and hugged me and kissed me. Then we all sat together and waited.

A doctor came and asked us to follow her. We went into a small room at the end of the corridor. She closed the door and asked us to sit down. She told us that they had operated to stop the bleeding in Sam's brain.

"When Sam hit his head on the concrete, it did a lot of damage to the back of his skull," the doctor said. "It was all made worse because he wasn't getting any oxygen when he was underwater. This meant that his heart stopped for a while." Then she looked at me. "He's lucky you were there and knew what to do."

Dad squeezed my hand.

"Anyway," the doctor went on, "Sam's stable at the moment but he's in a very serious condition. We're doing everything we can for him, but we'll need to see how things develop."

Mum asked if we could go and see him.

Sam was in a room in the ICU. We looked through a window at him. The light was low. The top of his head was bandaged and there was an oxygen mask over his mouth and nose so you couldn't see his face. There were drip tubes in his arms.

We stood there, too shocked to speak. Then Dad put his arm round me and Mum and led us out of the hospital.

Chapter 17
An Empty Shell

Sam was in a coma.

They took him off oxygen after four days because he could breathe by himself, but he didn't wake up.

He still didn't look like Sam – with the bandages on his head and the tubes going into him and out of him. And his pale grey skin. And the machine to measure his heart and pulse beeping away next to him.

He was alive, but this wasn't the Sam I knew – full of life and energy. He looked like an empty shell.

It hit Mum and Dad hard to see him like that. Mum started crying whenever she went into his room. Silent tears ran down her face until she had to leave and wait in the corridor. Dad didn't cry. He stared and shook his head, as if he couldn't believe what he was seeing.

They didn't speak to Sam and I couldn't understand why. All I wanted to do was talk to him.

Mum and Dad would only stay with him for a short time when we visited, then they left and waited for me in the café. I always got a chair then and sat close to Sam. I held his hand and talked to him for a few minutes. Just chat. Nothing serious. Just anything that came into my head. The weather. Books I was reading. Music I'd heard. Things I'd seen in the street.

I liked it best when I visited on my own. The hospital was only a 5-minute walk from school, so after the Christmas holidays I went every day on my way home before Mum and Dad got out of work.

I wasn't rushed when I was on my own. I could take my time and tell Sam all sorts of things. What I'd done. What I was happy about or worried about. Sometimes I told him that he had to get better. That he had to fight to wake up. And at the end of every visit, I told him what I'd never told him before – "I love you, Sam."

I didn't know if all this talking would make any difference. But I wanted to do it, and it felt right.

One day, a doctor came in and I stopped mid-sentence. But she had heard me and she said, "Don't stop. It's good for him."

"Do you think he can hear me?" I asked.

"What do you think?" she said.

"I think he can."

"So do I," she said. "So keep talking – I'm sure it helps."

That made me feel better, but I still never talked to Sam when Mum or Dad were there.

The only thing Dad ever said to Sam was 'Hello, son" when he arrived. Then he stood and stared out of the window as if it hurt too much to look at him.

Mum was different. She did nothing but look at Sam. She kissed his cheek and then held his hand and gazed at his face for the whole of her visits.

One day I went in and found that the nurses had taken Sam's bandages off. He looked much more like my brother now. I laughed and told him he needed a haircut. And I started to sing a silly old song I knew about a Long-Haired Lover from Liverpool.

I was holding Sam's hand as I sang and I was sure that I felt a twitch in his fingers – as if he was trying to tell me that he could hear.

Was it my imagination?

I sang the song again. But this time I didn't feel anything.

Sometimes in my bedroom I watched the video that Sam had made of me at the river. I could see the fear on my face as I'd made my way from one pillar to the next. And then I remembered how Sam had skipped across without a care in the world. It had been wild and exciting and beautiful the way he'd moved.

And now he was in a coma.

Maybe he would never wake up. I'd checked on the internet and found out that sometimes people stayed in a coma for ever. Maybe Sam would never run and jump again.

But I wouldn't let myself think like that. I would do everything I could to make him well again. I wouldn't mind if he teased me. I wouldn't mind if he was mean to me. I wanted to hear him laugh. I wanted to hear him swear. I wanted to see him drink too much. I wanted to see him wild and exciting again.

So I read to him. I took in my favourite book, started at page 1, and bit by bit I read the whole story. And I sang to him. If his eyes had been open I would even have danced for him. All the things he used to tease me about. He would probably have punched me in the face if he'd been awake. But he wasn't and so I kept on.

Chapter 18
Smile

I went to see Sam every day after school. For nearly five weeks he just lay there not moving while I talked or read to him or sang songs to him.

Then one day, I decided to sing 'You Stand By Me', the song that had won me the talent show. I knew Sam hated it and thought it was a crap song, but perhaps it would jog his memory. At the end of the song, I saw what looked like a little smile move across Sam's lips.

Was it my imagination or had Sam really smiled?

When one of the nurses came in I asked him to watch while I sang the song. But this time,

Sam's lips didn't move. I sang it again, louder. Still no movement.

The next day I sang the song again and asked Sam to smile. His lips moved and I felt a tiny squeeze of my hand.

"You can hear me, can't you, Sam?" I said. "You can, I know you can." He gave no sign, but I went on. "You've got to wake up, Sam. You've got to!"

At that moment Mum and Dad came in. I decided to try again, so I made them both hold Sam's hand. Then I sang the song to him.

Nothing.

"Come on, Sam – smile."

Nothing.

Maybe it was all in my imagination.

I sang the song again.

Nothing.

"Smile, Sam," I said. "I warn you – if you don't smile I'll sing that crap song again!"

It was a joke and Sam got it.

His lips twitched. A little upward curve. A smile.

And Mum and Dad both gasped as they felt a tiny squeeze of the hand.

No doubt about it. Sam had heard my joke. He could hear. He could understand. He had smiled.

Chapter 19

No Sport. No Girls. Nothing

Two days after he smiled at my joke, Sam opened his eyes.

He didn't look round or anything. He didn't seem to see us when we bent over him and said his name. But his eyes were open.

"Remember he's been in a coma for over a month," the doctor said. "He's very tired and in a confused state. I have to warn you – any recovery will be very slow."

The doctor was wrong.

When I went in the next day, Sam opened his eyes when I called his name and his eyes moved to look at me. And there was that little smile. He recognised me and I could see he was listening when I spoke to him.

From then on, there was progress every day. Within a week Sam was able to move his head and his fingers.

I went every day after school and I always read to him, so I remember his progress by the books I read.

While I was reading *To Kill a Mockingbird*, Sam started to talk. I went in one day and chatted a bit then I said, "Shall I go on with the book?" I looked at him to see if I could get an answer in his eyes or a nod of his head, but Sam took a deep breath and said, "Yes."

It was while we were reading *White Fang* that Sam was able to sit up in bed and start to use his arms.

We were reading *The Outsiders* when at last he got out of bed and sat in a chair.

Sam didn't just listen to the books. He discussed them with me. He didn't like this character, he liked that character, or he predicted how the story would turn out.

"Don't tell me what happens, Ben," he always said.

He never called me Chick now. Probably because Dad kept telling him how brave I'd been when I saved him. That made me cringe a bit but it made me pleased, too, of course.

I tried reading *Lord of the Rings* to Sam, but he said it was too slow and he preferred the films.

But he loved the *Sherlock Holmes* stories and after I'd read a couple of them he asked me to leave the book so that he could read them on his own.

For weeks Sam seemed to be getting better every day. Then the progress stopped.

He could talk, he could move everything in the upper part of his body, but his legs were still so weak that he couldn't stand or walk.

"I'll never walk again, Ben," he said one day when he'd been at the gym with the physio doing exercises to build up his leg muscles.

"Of course you will," I said.

"I know I won't," he said. "I'll be stuck in this wheelchair. No sport. No girls. Nothing."

"No girls" meant Holly. Sam hadn't said anything, but I knew he was hurt that she hadn't visited him.

I rang her one day and asked her to visit him.

She said she couldn't. When I asked why, she said she was going out with someone else.

I won't tell you the names I called her!

Chapter 20
Brothers

I didn't tell Sam about Holly, of course. But that phone call made me even more determined.

I wouldn't let Sam give up. I would make him learn to walk again.

In the summer holidays I was in the hospital nearly all day every day. We read together and I went to the gym with him, too. The physio showed me what exercises Sam had to do and I made him do them again when we got back to his room.

He read books on his own, but he still preferred me to read to him. So I started to blackmail him – I'd read a chapter if he did some of his exercises while I was reading.

"You're a bloody bully!" Sam would say. But I just laughed and made him do the exercises.

While I read, Sam massaged his leg muscles then lifted his feet a centimetre or two. Each day he could lift them a little bit higher.

Then he made a big step forward. At the end of one of our sessions in the gym he managed to stand up. He wobbled a bit and he had to sit down almost at once, but he had stood up.

The next day he stood up again. And he was on his feet long enough to crack a huge grin and pump the air in triumph.

Sam was still grinning when I wheeled him back to his room. As I helped him out of the wheelchair, he grabbed my hand.

"Thanks, Ben," he said.

"What for?"

"For everything."

All the next week Sam finished the gym sessions by standing, and every day he managed to stand for longer.

"How about trying a couple of steps?" I said to him one day when we got back from the gym.

"No, go on – read the book. I want to know what happens to them."

We were reading *Of Mice and Men* and he was really caught up in the story of Lennie and George.

"I'll read right to the end if you try to walk a couple of steps," I said.

"No!" Sam said.

He stood up and tried to grab the book from my hand. I moved back out of reach.

"Oh come on, Ben – read it!"

"No, you come on," I said. "Come on and get the book if you want it so much. Just a couple of steps."

Sam shook his head.

"Why not?" I asked.

He looked me in the eye and told me the truth, "I'm scared."

I knew how hard it must have been for him to say it. But he had changed so much and we were so close now. I could have cried but I laughed.

"Don't be a wimp!" I said.

He pointed his finger at me. "You're the wimp, not me," he said.

"Not any more," I said. "Come on, Sam. Two steps. Two steps today. Three tomorrow. Four the day after. Do it and you'll walk out of this place in a month. I promise."

"No way," Sam said.

"You will. The physio told me that once you start to walk nothing can stop your recovery. You'll be running in three months and back playing sport by the end of the year."

"Really? The physio said that?" he asked.

"Really. I promise you, Sam."

"Playing sport?" he said.

"Playing sport, chasing girls, whatever you want."

"You're not lying?"

"Cross my heart," I said. "But you've got to take those first steps. Come on, Sam – try! Do it for me."

He nodded.

I saw him clench his fist and screw his face up as he made the effort to move his leg forward.

"I can't," he said and I could see the fear in his eyes.

"Yes you can. You can! Just two steps," I said. And then I hit him with it. "I dare you."

Those three words.

Sam knew what I was doing. His mouth twisted into a smile. "OK," he said.

He clenched his fists and took a step.

"I did it!" he said as he grabbed hold of my hand.

"Of course you did!" I said. "I bet you can't do another one."

"Oh yeah? Watch me," Sam said.

And he took another step.

Then another.

Then another.

"OK, OK, now you're just showing off!" I said.

Sam started to laugh and I joined in. And soon we couldn't stop. We held onto each other and laughed louder and louder. We laughed because we were happy. And we laughed because we were relieved. And we laughed because Sam was going to walk again. And we laughed because life was great.

Everything was different. He had changed and so had I. We were equals now. Brothers. Proper brothers.

Our books are tested
for children and young people by
children and young people.

Thanks to everyone who consulted on
a manuscript for their time and effort in
helping us to make our books better
for our readers.